The WEREWOLF CLUB

Meets the Hound of the Basketballs

DANIEL AND JILL PINKWATER

ATHENEUM BOOKS FOR YOUNG READERS
New York London Toronto Sydney Singapore

Atheneum Books for Young Readers
An imprint of Simon & Schuster Children's Publishing Division
1230 Avenue of the Americas, New York, New York 10020

Text copyright © 2001 by Daniel Pinkwater
Illustrations © 2001 by Jill Pinkwater

Book design by Lisa Vega
The text of this book is set in Weidemann Book.
Printed in the United States of America
10 9 8 7 6 5 4 3 2 1

Library of Congress Cataloging-in-Publication Data:
Pinkwater, Daniel Manus, 1941-
The Werewolf Club meets the Hound of the Basketballs / Daniel and Jill Pinkwater.
p. cm.
The Werewolf Club ; #4
ISBN 0-689-84473-5 (pbk.)
Summary: The Watson Elementary School Werewolf Club goes on a field trip to Basketball Hall, where Sir Hugo hopes they will solve the mystery of the hound which has plagued his family for generations.
1. Werewolves—Fiction. 2. Mystery and detective stories. 3. Humorous stories.
Pinkwater, Jill. Pinkwater, Daniel Manus, 1941- Werewolf Club ; #4.
PZ7.P6335Wf 2001
[Fic]—dc21
2001035541
ISBN 0-689-84575-8

FIRST EDITION

CHAPTER ONE

The members of the Watson Elementary School Werewolf Club were having grilled cheese sandwiches at Honest Tom's Tibetan-American Lunchroom. Ralf Alfa, the handsome and athletic natural leader of the Werewolf Club, was having grilled American cheese on white bread. Lucy Fang, the most feared member of the Werewolf Club, was having grilled Swiss cheese on rye. I, Norman Gnormal, was having grilled Swiss cheese on whole wheat. I'm the newest member of the Werewolf Club. My parents really wanted a dog, not a kid, and raised me as a puppy; I only recently graduated from acting like a dog to actually becoming a werewolf.

Billy Furball, the least sanitary werewolf, was

1

having grilled Norwegian goat cheese, with herring bits, on Scandinavian health toast. Henry Count Dorkula wasn't a werewolf, but claimed to be some sort of vampire, so he hung out with us, since there wasn't a vampire club. Henry was having grilled cream cheese on raisin toast and a large tomato juice, which he drank through two straws.

Mr. Talbot, the faculty sponsor of the Werewolf Club, came into the restaurant all excited. "We've been invited! All of us! We're invited to visit my Uncle Hugo at his country house, Basketball Hall!"

"Yay!" the werewolves shouted.

"It's a basketball hall? Do we get to play?"

"Not exactly," Mr. Talbot said. "That's its name, Basketball Hall."

CHAPTER TWO

"Basketball Hall? But it's not a gym or a sports stadium, just a house?"

"Uncle Hugo's house. It's on the moor."

"Moor?"

"What moor?"

"Please sir, I want some moor?"

"I never heard of any moor."

"I heard that less is moor."

"What's a moor?"

[moor **1**: *chiefly Brit*: an expanse of open rolling infertile land

2: a boggy area of wasteland usu. peaty and dominated by grasses and sedges]

CHAPTER THREE

It was no trouble getting permission from our parents. They liked it when the Werewolf Club went on field trips because it gave them a chance to hose down our rooms, throw out some of the older chew-bones, and vacuum the fur out of the rugs.

Mr. Talbot borrowed Principal Pantaloni's van. We loaded up with soda and snacks and headed for the open road. Henry Count Dorkula, the vampire who hung around with the Werewolf Club because there wasn't a vampire club, was with us. He led us in songs:

"100 bottles of blood on the wall"

"There was a vampire had a bat and Bingo was his name-o"

5

"Eensy beensy spider—I ate it"

Henry Count Dorkula was not the traditional blood-drinking kind of vampire. He was more of a fruit bat, but he kept up the old traditions.

We had fun riding and singing and eating snacks. Billy Furball got carsick, several times. We cheered and clapped.

Billy Furball never disappoints us.

CHAPTER FOUR

"Do you know how to find Basketball Hall?" we asked Mr. Talbot.

"More or less," Mr. Talbot said. "When we get into the general neighborhood, we can ask a local yokel."

"Look!" Lucy Fang said.

We passed a sign:

5 Miles to the Local Yokel

"Is that the local yokel you're going to ask for directions?" Ralf Alfa asked.

After a while there was another sign:

> **Just 2 Miles to the Local Yokel**

"The yokel puts up signs?" Billy Furball asked. "I guess he gets asked directions a lot."

Another sign:

> **One Mile! One Mile to the Local Yokel!**

Then there was another sign:

> **Local Yokel 1/2 Mile!**

And then:

> **Slow Down! Slow Down! 1000 Yards to the Local Yokel!**

CHAPTER FIVE

Then we saw it—a wooden building shaped like a barn. There was a big sign on top:

Local Yokel Diner—We Have Jitterbugs

"Hey! They have jitterbugs!" Mr. Talbot said. "We should stop here."

A jitterbug, we soon found out, is the name of a gourmet specialty. This is how it is made: You take a nice, soft, spongy slice of packaged white bread and put it on a plate. On top of that you put either a slice of meatloaf or a hamburger. Then, on top of that, you put a scooped mound of mashed potatoes. You make a dent on top of the mound with the scooper you scooped it with, and then you pour brown gravy all over the thing. It puddles up in the dent. As I said, a gourmet specialty.

A greasy, soggy gourmet specialty. Mr. Talbot said he used to have them all the time when he was a boy in Poughkeepsie, New York. He ordered six of them—one for each member of the Werewolf Club, and one for himself. Then he ate them all—except Billy Furball's. Billy Furball said his jitterbug was pretty good.

CHAPTER SIX

A man in a white apron approached us.

"Is everything satisfactory?" he asked. "I am Local W. Yokel, owner and proprietor of the Local Yokel Diner, newsstand, and bus stop."

"I am Lawrence Talbot, elementary school teacher, and these are some of my pupils," Mr. Talbot said. "I was hoping to ask you . . . do you know the way to Basketball Hall?"

"Arrr, be ye not planning to go to the Hall?" Local W. Yokel said.

"Yes," Mr. Talbot said. "Why shouldn't we? And why are you suddenly saying things like, 'Arrr' and 'be ye'?"

"Arrr. Some say the Hall be an evil place," Local W. Yokel said.

"Local Yokel is nutty as a fruitcake, isn't he?" Lucy Fang asked.

"Arrr. And they don't have cable."

We agreed that he seemed to be.

Along with telling us all sorts of mixed-up things about strange goings-on, Sir Hugo, ghostly hounds, and haunted pastrami, and going 'Arrr' a lot, the Local Yokel did mention what road to take, so Mr. Talbot paid for the jitterbugs and we left.

CHAPTER SEVEN

In the van Mr. Talbot said, "Fie, faugh, fooey, and feh! I don't believe in such balderdash."

"Balderdash?" said Ralf.

"Old wives' and local yokels' tales. Superstition, witches and fairies, goblins, enormous hounds, magical pastrami. It's all a lot of applesauce."

"Mr. Talbot, you yourself are a werewolf," Lucy pointed out.

"So?"

"We are all werewolves, except Henry, who is a vampire, and possibly Norman, who wasn't formerly a werewolf, but may be one now," she went on.

"And your point is?"

"Shouldn't you be a little more open-minded?"

13

"Why?"

"Well, there are people who wouldn't believe in us."

"Being a werewolf is a normal, healthy thing. This haunted pastrami stuff is sick."

CHAPTER EIGHT

We arrived at Basketball Hall. It was old-looking and scary and spooky. It looked like something out of a horror movie. There were towers, and bats flying around. There was a big iron fence all around it.

"This is cool," Billy Furball said.

We all agreed that it was.

Sir Hugo came out to meet us. He looked a little like Mr. Talbot, his nephew, only he was neater, and of course, he wasn't a werewolf.

"Thank you for coming, Nephew," Sir Hugo said. "I've ordered the chef to prepare liver treats for everyone."

"If you're Mr. Talbot's uncle, how come you have a different last name?" Billy Furball asked.

"It's a different branch of the family. The Basketballs go back a long way."

"And you've always lived in Basketball Hall?" Billy Furball asked.

"It's named in honor of the first Sir Hugo," Sir Hugo said. "He was rather round, and dribbled a lot."

CHAPTER NINE

"Let me show you around Basketball Hall," Sir Hugo said. "It was built by the famous architects Burke and Hare. If you go up into the tower, you can see Yonkers."

Sir Hugo led us through the drafty rooms of Basketball Hall. There was a lot of beat-up old furniture from the Middle Ages and paintings so dark we couldn't see what they were about.

"You sure have a lot of old relics, Sir Hugo," Billy Furball said.

"Old relics?" Sir Hugo asked. "I suppose I have. Speaking of which, here are Mr. and Mrs. Barrymore, my servants . . . Barry Barrymore and Mary Barrymore. They are what are known as 'old retainers.' And," Sir Hugo whispered behind his hand, "you will notice that Mr. Barrymore wears an old retainer. It was given to him by old Dr. Dell, the dentist in the dell."

We werewolves were confused by Sir Hugo's obscure joke and also fascinated by the Barrymores, who were old and repulsive—so, naturally we liked them.

"These young werewolves are my guests and must be shown every courtesy," Sir Hugo said. "Lawrence Talbot is my nephew, as you know."

Mary Barrymore threw herself upon Mr. Talbot and began to weep. "Oh, Mr. Larry, it does an old retainer's heart good to see you again so fat and healthy after all these years! Things have been hard at Basketball Hall. Mr. Barrymore talks in his sleep. He has some guilty secret. I cry all the time. Sir Hugo locks himself in his room every night and sometimes we hear Miss Glucinda screaming. I often suspect that something is wrong."

"Just like when I was a boy!" Mr. Talbot said. "I used to come here in the summers. It's a fun place."

"Who's Miss Glucinda?" I asked.

CHAPTER TEN

We heard a scream. We all looked up. There at the top of the stairs stood a girl. She had hair like spun gold. She had skin like ivory. She had teeth like pearls. Her eyes were of the deepest blue. Otherwise she looked a lot like Mr. Talbot. We could not help but stare.

"Even I am slightly revolted," Billy Furball whispered.

"What? Have you no eyes?" Henry Count Dorkula whispered. "That is one hot mama."

"My niece, Miss Glucinda," Sir Hugo said. "One day Basketball Hall will be hers."

"Why did she scream?" Mr. Talbot whispered to Mrs. Barrymore, who was still hugging him and weeping softly.

"She has some secret sorrow," Mrs. Barrymore said, "or possibly I have once again put way too much starch in her underwear. I have become forgetful in my old years."

Miss Glucinda descended the staircase. "Uncle," she said in a tragic tone, "who are these . . . people?"

"You remember your cousin, Lawrence Talbot," Sir Hugo said. "And these young people are some of his pupils."

"But they are vulgar, coarse young people, and they smell of wolf spit," Miss Glucinda said. "Except this one. What is your name?" she asked Henry Count Dorkula.

Henry Count Dorkula bowed and kissed Miss Glucinda's hand. "I am Henry Count Dorkula. In my veins runs the blood of Rumanian noblemen."

"Rumania? Isn't that where pastrami comes from? Come," Miss Glucinda said, "we will speak more."

"Yahoo! Yum-yum! Hubba-hubba! Whoopee!" Henry Count Dorkula said.

CHAPTER ELEVEN

"Our guests must be hungry," Sir Hugo said. "Mr. Barrymore, I believe it is all-you-can-eat knackwurst and sauerkraut night at the Local Yokel Diner. Drive down and get ten orders, then come back and keep your motor running in case we want more. Mrs. Barrymore, perhaps you should go with him to make sure he doesn't forget the extra-hot, green horseradish sauce."

"Wasabi?" Mr. Talbot asked.

"Gesundheit!" said Sir Hugo.

Mr. and Mrs. Barrymore motored off in Sir Hugo's stately Wartburg limousine.

"I'm sure a few orders of knackwurst and sauerkraut won't go amiss," said Uncle Hugo, "but the real reason I sent them away was in order to speak to you without being overheard. You see, I know of your recent success in dealing with the meatball-like space aliens."

"I ate a whole psychiatrist," Billy Furball said.

"Just so. And also the fruit vampire you defeated."

"That was Noshferatu, Henry Count Dorkula's great-great-great-great-uncle," Mr. Talbot said. "He took quite a bit of defeating. By the way, where is Henry?"

We heard a scream from somewhere deep within the great house.

"That sounds like Henry now," Ralf Alfa said. "He went off with Miss Glucinda."

"You other children can tell him later what I'm about to tell you," said Sir Hugo.

"What about the fact that we just heard Henry scream?" asked Lucy Fang.

"Miss Glucinda tends to cause people to scream," her uncle said. "It's just something about her. I'm sure they're having a nice time."

CHAPTER TWELVE

"You see," Sir Hugo continued, "I did not invite you here just for a visit. I'm hoping you can help me with a serious problem. My father, Sir Lugo Basketball, received a great fright. It was the last fright of his life. Something so frightening that he was never to see daylight again."

"Something frightened him so badly?" Mr. Talbot asked. "Frightened him to death?"

"Oh, no," said Sir Hugo, "not frightened to death. He's quite alive." Sir Hugo opened a cupboard. Crouching inside was an old man with the usual Basketball/Talbot features.

"He was just so frightened that he never saw daylight again. Papa has been in this cupboard for

well over a year. Isn't that right, Papa?"

"Close the door, Sonny," Sir Lugo Basketball said. "I don't want that thing to find me."

Sir Hugo closed the cupboard door.

"What was it that frightened him so?" Mr. Talbot asked.

"He refuses to say," Sir Hugo replied, "but when we found him all curled up and chewing on his fingernails—and he had wet his pants too—all around him were the enormous footprints of a hound."

"How long before the Barrymores get back with the knackwurst and sauerkraut?" Billy Furball asked.

CHAPTER THIRTEEN

"It gets pretty crazy on all-you-can-eat knackwurst and sauerkraut night, but I expect my retainers will return any minute. And now, while we wait, I wish to tell you the legend of the Hound of the Basketballs."

Just then we heard another bloodcurdling scream.

"Wow!" Ralf Alfa said. "That darn near curdled my blood. Who did that?"

We looked up, and there we saw Henry Count Dorkula standing at the top of the stairs.

"Did you do that?" Lucy Fang asked. "Did you scream?"

"Yes," Henry Count Dorkula said. "It's something I picked up from Miss Glucinda. It's therapeutic. It makes me feel all free." He screamed again.

"Stop doing that," Billy Furball said. "It dulls my appetite. Besides, Sir Hugo was just about to tell us the legend of the Hound of the Basketballs."

There was another scream. It was Miss Glucinda. She was holding a large, old book. "The Hound!" she screamed. "I have the legend here!"

Henry Count Dorkula came down the stairs first.

"How's it going with Miss Glucinda?" Ralf Alfa whispered.

"I've been bitten," Henry Count Dorkula whispered back.

"Bitten? By the love bug?" Ralf Alfa asked.

"No, bitten by Miss Glucinda," Henry Count Dorkula said. "She nipped me a good one on the ankle."

CHAPTER FOURTEEN

"Now we get to see Henry turn into a Miss Glucinda," Lucy Fang said.

"That sort of thing is just folklore," Mr. Talbot said.

"But isn't that one of the ways to become a werewolf?" asked Ralf Alfa.

"Maybe. I don't know. I have personal problems. Don't you children understand? I can't handle all this responsibility," Mr. Talbot whined.

"I think he's getting cranky," Billy Furball said. "We should feed him."

"The Barrymores haven't returned with the knackwurst yet. We are foodless. Maybe hearing about the legend of the Hound of the Basketballs will calm him down," said Lucy Fang.

"Good-o. I will tell the tale," said Sir Hugo. "And don't any of you ravenous, caninelike beings fret. The food will be arriving shortly."

Sir Hugo sat down in an enormous armchair and began to speak.

"No way, Uncle," Miss Glucinda interrupted. "I have the book and I'm going to tell the tale."

Miss Glucinda sat down on the bottom step of the winding staircase and opened the large book she was carrying.

"There seems to be some sort of poem or lyric first. It's not printed. It's all written in by hand.

"In the good old colony days,
When we lived under the king,
Lived a fiendish Hound
Who was low to the ground—
A spooky, scary thing.

Sir Hugo was a rat.
He was ugly, mean, and fat.
He was chased by the Hound

Who hunted him down
And bit him where he sat.

Sir Hugo was a louse.
He lived in a big house.
Along came the Hound,
Making horrible sounds,
And punched him in the mouth."

Billy Furball asked, "What is it, some kind of old song?"

"I guess so," Miss Glucinda said. "It goes on:

"There will always be a Hound
That lives upon the moor;
It will always pound
Sir Hugo's butt
When he goes out of doors."

"It doesn't make any sense to me," Miss Glucinda said, "even though we read it every St. Melvin's Day."

"Perhaps it will make sense as we go along. What comes next?" Mr. Talbot asked.

"This appears to be an older manuscript that's glued in," said Miss Glucinda.

CHAPTER FIFTEEN

"'Know then that in the time when our colony was newly settled, Sir Hugo Basketball, a wild, profane, and godless man, did do many naughty things to the common folk and tradespeople of the town,'" Miss Glucinda read out loud.

"That would be my ancestor, the first Sir Hugo," Sir Hugo said.

"Did he do naughty things?" Lucy Fang said.

"Old-fashioned English," Mr. Talbot said. "Please continue, Miss Glucinda."

"'So wicked and naughty was Sir Hugo that the people of the parish feared his evil name. Especially after he did do particularly awful things to some yeomen of the locality. He was found most horribly dead and also chewed upon with spit all over him. And in the earth about his body were seen the gigantic footprints of a hound. Here ends the legend of the Hound of the Basketballs,'" Miss Glucinda finished.

"Wow, some bloodcurdling legend," Ralf Alfa said.

"When do we eat?" Billy Furball asked.

The Barrymores burst into the room carrying stacks of plastic foam containers.

"Who wants knackwurst?" shouted Mr. Barry Barrymore.

CHAPTER SIXTEEN

The Werewolf Club, Sir Hugo, Miss Glucinda, and the Barrymores made short work of the knackwurst and sauerkraut.

"I'm still hungry," Billy Furball said.

"It's all-you-can-eat night at the Local Yokel Diner," Sir Hugo shouted. "Barrymore! Drive back and get seconds for everyone."

"Right!" Barry Barrymore said. "And this time I'll bring pumpkin pies, too."

We heard the mighty diesel engine of the Wartburg limousine rattle down the drive as the Barrymores headed for the Local Yokel Diner to bring us even more yummy knackwurst and hot, steaming sauerkraut.

"So what was all this reading of the legend about?" Mr. Talbot asked Sir Hugo.

"Was it not of interest?" Sir Hugo asked.

"Maybe if I were a collector of fairy tales," Mr. Talbot said. "What does it all mean?"

"It means," said Sir Hugo, "that the Hound of the Basketballs is real. He exists to this day . . . and every master of Basketball Hall since the time of the first Sir Hugo has been chased, pounced upon, chewed upon, gotten spit all over him, or WORSE . . . because of the accursed Hound."

"Have you seen him?" asked Mr. Talbot.

"I have felt his evil breath," Sir Hugo said, "which smelled a bit like knackwurst, now that I think of it."

"Very interesting," said Mr. Talbot.

"If we should want thirds of the knackwurst and sauerkraut," Billy Furball asked, "would the Barrymores be willing to go back to the Local Yokel Diner?"

"I can arrange for them to drive you there," Sir Hugo said, "and wait until you eat your fill."

"Oh, boy," Billy Furball said.

"I should tell you," Mr. Talbot said, "Billy's the one who ate an entire space alien by himself."

"I know this," Sir Hugo said. "There is a good-natured rivalry between the Local Yokel and myself. I would like it if young Billy Furball broke the bank."

CHAPTER SEVENTEEN

"So, let me get this straight. You invited us here not just because you like us . . .," Mr. Talbot began.

"Of course I like you, Nephew," Sir Hugo said. "And now that I've met these young people, I like them very much as well."

"I like Henry," Miss Glucinda said.

"But it is true," Sir Hugo said, "I did not invite you here just because I like you."

"Nor did you invite us just to give us unlimited knackwurst and sauerkraut."

"This too is true," Sir Hugo said. "Though I am happy, of course, to feed my guests."

"Next time the Barrymores are going to drive me

39

to the Local Yokel," Billy Furball said. "And I will eat every knackwurst in the place."

"We will all come along to see that," Sir Hugo said.

CHAPTER EIGHTEEN

"All right, you did not invite us just because you like us. You did not invite us here just to give us knackwurst," Mr. Talbot said. "Clearly you invited us here because you want something done about . . . THE HOUND."

"You said it, Buster," Sir Hugo said. "Only you and the rest of your pupils, the darling little werewolves, can solve the mystery that has plagued Basketball Hall.

"Miss Glucinda, continue reading from the great book!"

Miss Glucinda opened the old book and read:

> *"Ye Hound is cometh when the moon*
> *be fulleth.*

41

Only when the moon be round
Doth the people see ye Hound.

When ye moon be big and bright
Get ye ready to take a bite.

Be ye cruel or be ye kind
The Hound will bite thy sorry behind.

The Hound shall biteth one and all
But most of all Sir Basketball."

Miss Glucinda slammed the book shut.

"So what we have here," Sir Hugo said, "is a supernatural hound that roams the moors by moonlight scaring people and especially biting members of the Basketball family. Which includes you, Nephew, so watch your hindquarters."

"And according to my pocket calendar," Mr. Talbot said, "there's a full moon tonight, and you expect my pupils and me to change into werewolves and make ourselves useful on the moors."

"Exactly," said Sir Hugo. "If a bunch of were-wolves can't catch the Hound, then I'm a Dutchman."

CHAPTER NINETEEN

"I'm still hungry," Billy Furball said.

"Wait outside," Sir Hugo said. "When the Barrymores return, tell them to drive you to the Local Yokel Diner, where you can eat until you faint."

"Really?" Billy Furball trotted off to the front door.

"I thought you wanted to watch the disgusting spectacle yourself," Mr. Talbot muttered.

Sir Hugo ignored him. "Tell the Barrymores to put the knackwurst and sauerkraut they have fetched into the larder before driving you," Sir Hugo called after Billy Furball.

Then to us he said, "I suspect appetites will be rather keen later on."

"Why did you send Billy Furball away? Now

we're short a werewolf for the hunt," Mr. Talbot said.

"He will distract the old Barrymores who, for some reason, seem to get in the way in matters concerning the horrible Hound."

"Why don't you and I go to the tower? There's a good view of the moor from up there, and I have a pair of Japanese naval binoculars." Miss Glucinda flashed her pearly white teeth at Henry Count Dorkula.

"Why not? Not much a bat can do in a hound hunt," Henry Count Dorkula said, following Miss Glucinda up the winding stairs.

"Hey, Cape Boy, what about aerial reconnaissance? What about flybys and flyovers and all that good stuff? And don't bats have radar? You could save us lots of time," Lucy Fang shouted.

But Henry Count Dorkula wasn't listening. In a minute he was out of sight. This was typical. We werewolves were never sure about whether he was able to turn into a bat. Sometimes we thought we had seen him do it, and other times, we thought we hadn't.

"Look! The moon!" Ralf Alfa said. We werewolves felt the first tingle of fur sprouting all over our bodies. Our noses stretched, and our fingernails turned into powerful claws.

"Awoo!" I said.

"Awoo!" Lucy Fang, Ralf Alfa, and Mr. Talbot said.

Seated at the counter of the Local Yokel Diner, eating his fourth refill of knackwurst and sauerkraut, Billy Furball said, "Awoo!"

In the tower Henry Count Dorkula and Miss Glucinda watched the moon rise over the moor. "I'm going to change! I'm going to change!" Miss Glucinda said abruptly.

"You're going to change into a werewolf?" Henry Count Dorkula asked.

Miss Glucinda didn't seem to hear him. "I'm going to change! I'm going to change!" she repeated.

Henry tried again. "You're not going to change into a vampire bat, are you?"

"I'm going to change! I'm going to change!" Miss Glucinda jumped up and ran out of the room.

It seemed only moments before Miss Glucinda returned.

"I changed," she said. "Do you like my evening

gown? It's so romantic up here in the tower."

"You're not going to bite me again, are you?" Henry asked.

"Not right now. Let's watch the action on the moor."

CHAPTER TWENTY

The moon had risen. The members of the Werewolf Club minus one—well, two if you count Henry—had transformed. We were long-legged wolves and we had a purpose. We howled, we stretched, we sniffed the air, and then, all at once, something struck us. We leaped into the air and headed onto the flat plain.

Billy Furball sat at the counter of the Local Yokel Diner and ate. And ate. And ate. Mr. Local Yokel, proprietor of the Local Yokel Diner, watched in amazement as he scooped the last of the knackwurst from the bottom of the huge pot.

"Aren't you a lot more hairy than when you came in, and aren't you feeling even a little sick?" he asked Billy Furball. "You're flirting with knackwurst poisoning, you know."

Billy Furball burped and smiled. "More?" he asked.

"All gone," Mr. Yokel said.

"All gone?" Billy Furball asked.

"Finished. Done. Cleaned out. You broke the knackwurst bank, kid."

The other patrons, who had been watching the ghastly spectacle, cheered.

"Never saw the like," one of the regulars said.

"Not in person," said another.

"Oh, you mean those strange people from the Hall?"

"Basketball Hall?" Billy Furball asked.

"Yeah. The ones outside who are putting the bags of knackwurst and sauerkraut in the trunk of their car. They do that every week."

"Do what?" Billy Furball asked.

"Come in on all-you-can-eat night and then come back for seconds and thirds and fourths."

"Before you, they were the knackwurst- and sauerkraut-eating champions. But they never consume on the premises. We operate on the honor system, so I assume they're eating everything . . . still, it's not the same," Mr. Yokel said. "Say, kid, you're not moving into the neighborhood, are you?"

"Just visiting," Billy Furball said.

"Have room for a piece of pie?" Mr. Yokel asked. "My treat."

Billy Furball was finishing his pie when Mr. Barry Barrymore tapped him on the shoulder. "Ready to leave, young master?"

When the Wartburg limousine pulled up in front of Basketball Hall, Billy Furball said, "You know, I could eat just one more knackwurst. You don't happen to have a few rattling around, do you?"

"We have no more knackwurst and sauerkraut, young sir," Mr. Barry Barrymore replied. "You ate all there was. We will say good night and retire to our quarters."

"Hmm," said Billy Furball, sniffing the air. Probably even without his werewolf nose he would have detected the containers of knackwurst and sauerkraut locked in the trunk of the car. But he said nothing.

They may just be knackwurst rustlers, he thought. *No reason to embarrass them.*

CHAPTER TWENTY-ONE

We werewolves raced to the north. We stopped and flung our great noses into the air. We sniffed deeply. Then we raced to the south. We heard a strange, unearthly sound. We stopped. We listened. We sniffed again. Finally, we smelled it. Then we saw it.

It was a small, roly-poly animal with knackwurst on its breath.

"I think the werewolves have found something," Henry Count Dorkula said, peering through the Japanese naval binoculars. "It's! It's! No, wait . . . it's just some little dog. Hey! Quit biting me!"

CHAPTER TWENTY-TWO

"Look what we found," Lucy Fang announced as the Werewolf Club entered the Hall.

"The Hound! The Hound!" Sir Hugo screamed in terror as he pointed to the small, fat dog.

Sir Hugo's father, hearing his son's cries of panic, stuck his head out of his cupboard, took a quick look, and said, "Yep, that's it." The old man ducked back into the cupboard and slammed the door.

"This is the Hound? This is what you're afraid of?" Lucy Fang said as she nuzzled the fat dog she was carrying. "It's not much bigger than a pussycat."

"It's the Hound and we're scared of it!" Sir Hugo said. "It's an unearthly being. Just look at that vicious expression."

"Aw . . . so cute," Ralf Alfa said.

"This is what you dragged us here for?" Mr. Talbot asked.

"The knackwurst and sauerkraut were very good," Billy Furball said.

"You're back. Where are those Barrymores?" Sir Hugo demanded.

"Probably looking for this dog so they can feed it knackwurst and sauerkraut," Billy Furball said.

"What do you mean?" I asked.

"I can smell the knackwurst on its breath from here," Billy Furball said.

"We can too. Does that have something do with the Barrymores?" Mr. Talbot asked.

Billy Furball told everyone what he had heard at the Local Yokel Diner. "I heard they're heavy hitters on the honor system every all-you-can-eat knackwurst and sauerkraut night. Also, they brought a trunkload of knackwurst back tonight and denied having done so."

"My loyal retainers have been getting limitless quantities of knackwurst and sauerkraut every week? To feed the evil Hound?" Sir Hugo roared.

CHAPTER TWENTY-THREE

"How could you do this?" Sir Hugo asked. "How could you secretly feed and encourage the Hound, known to be a curse on every generation of Basketballs?"

"Well, Your Lordship," Old Barry Barrymore began, "there have been Barrymores looking after the lord of Basketball Hall for some hundreds of years, have there not?"

"Yes. This is true," Sir Hugo said.

"And the Barrymores have never liked the lords of Basketball Hall, is that not so, Sir Hugo?"

"Also true," Sir Hugo said. "And we have never much liked the Barrymores. They smell of knackwurst, for one thing. By Jove! Knackwurst!"

"The secret of breeding the Basketball Hound,"

old Mary Barrymore said. "Knackwurst, and plenty of it. Makes them gassy and frightening."

"I don't think this sweet pup is frightening," Lucy Fang said.

"But you will admit it's gassy, my dear," Mary Barrymore said.

"Let's open some windows," Ralf Alfa said.

CHAPTER TWENTY-FOUR

"And the purpose of all this is to scare us into having heart failure, am I right?" Sir Hugo asked.

"No, it's just to annoy you," Barry Barrymore said. "Over the decades the hatred-to-the-death thing has sort of eroded to practical jokes and reading your mail."

The moon was setting, and those of us who were werewolves were returning to more or less human form.

"It will soon be dawn," Mr. Talbot said. "Our work here is done."

"This was the best trip I ever took in my life," Billy Furball said.

"So, can we keep the Hound right here in the hall?" the Barrymores asked.

"No!" shouted Sir Lugo from inside the cupboard.

"I have bruises from where Miss Glucinda bit me," Henry Count Dorkula said.

"We will go home now, Uncle," Mr. Talbot said. "We are glad we were able to solve this mystery."

"That is the worst-smelling hound I have ever encountered," said Sir Hugo.

"The Barrymores have invited me to come and visit them during the summer," Billy Furball said.

"That's nice, Billy," we all said.

END